MISSIONS OF THE U.S.
GREEN BERETS

BY BRANDON TERRELL

Published by The Child's World®
1980 Lookout Drive • Mankato, MN 56003-1705
800-599-READ • www.childsworld.com

Acknowledgments
The Child's World®: Mary Berendes, Publishing Director
Red Line Editorial: Design, editorial direction, and production
Photographs ©: U.S. Army, cover, 1; Spc. Joseph A. Wilson/U.S. Army, 5;
Spc. Steven K. Young/U.S. Army, 6; U.S. Air Force/USAF National Museum
of the Air Force, 8; Bettmann/Corbis, 10; South Carolina National Guard,
12; Tech. Sgt. Matt Hecht/U.S. Air National Guard, 14, 20; Vladislav Gajic/
Shutterstock Images, 16; Darren Brode/Shutterstock Images, 17; Pfc. Andrew
Vidakovich, 18

ISBN 9781634074445

LCCN 2015946358

Printed in the United States of America
Mankato, MN
December, 2015
PA02285

TABLE OF
CONTENTS

ABOUT THE U.S. GREEN BERETS

- The Green Berets are officially known as the United States Army Special Forces.

- The Special Forces program began in 1952.

- A basic unit in the Green Berets includes 12 soldiers. This group is called an A-Team.

- A Special Forces company consists of six A-Teams.

- U.S. President John F. Kennedy wanted Special Forces to have something to set them apart. He suggested they wear green berets. Operational Detachment FA-32 was a single team. These team members were the first to wear the signature green beret during training exercises.

- A common weapon of the Green Berets is the MP-5 submachine gun.

- The Green Beret motto is *De Oppresso Liber*, which is Latin for "To Free the Oppressed."

CHAPTER 1

GREEN BERETS TRAINING

With his signature hat perched on his head, the Green Beret ranking officer stared at a new **recruit**. "Welcome to the United States Army Special Forces," the officer said gruffly. The commanding officer stood face-to-face with the new soldier. "Think you have what it takes to become a Green

Beret?" he asked. "Berets are the best of the best. It takes a lot of hard work to earn that title."

The officer ran down the list of things recruits must do to be considered for the Berets. Special Forces members must be able to handle extreme situations. This includes hunger, rough weather, and extreme tiredness. They must pass parachute training.

Recruits must first handle a difficult test. It is a test of strength and determination. The test lasts three weeks. It is called the Special Forces Assessment and Selection Course, or SFAS.

The officer was still circling the recruit. He wanted to see if the recruit would break. The recruit stood tall and stiff. He didn't move. Not even when the officer listed the tests he would face. Less than three to five hours of sleep each night. Swimming 164 feet (50 m) while wearing full uniform and boots. Doing push-ups and sit-ups. Running 2 miles (3.2 km). Climbing ropes and a 7-foot (2-m) wall. The SFAS is just the beginning. The Green Berets carry out some of the most difficult and dangerous missions.

"So I repeat," said the officer, "do you think you have the courage and the strength to be a Green Beret?"

"Sir, yes, sir!" the recruit shouted.

CHAPTER 2

OPERATION KINGPIN

It was 1970 in Vietnam. There was little room to land a helicopter at Son Tay, a prison camp. The pilot had no choice. The chopper carrying 20 Green Berets crashed inside the camp's grounds.

Rat-a-tat-a-tat!

Large U.S. Navy helicopters fired their guns at the enemy guard towers. The Berets could hear explosions in the distance. More aircraft shot down bridges. This would keep the enemy's help from making it to the prison.

More than 350 Americans had been taken prisoner in North Vietnam. Most of them were pilots. The conditions were terrible. Nobody on the outside knew there were men being held **hostage**. That all changed with one photograph.

A video taken from an aircraft showed two prisoner camps. The camps were near the city of Hanoi. Someone in the aircraft snapped a grainy photograph. In the dirt, the prisoners had written the letter K. It was code that meant "Come get us." And that was just what the Green Berets planned to do.

Lieutenant Arthur "Bull" Simons led the team of Green Berets. They spent months preparing for the mission. They even built a model of the prison. This helped them practice their plan. On the night of November 20, just hours before the operation began, Simons told his team the truth behind their mission. He told them they would be saving 70 people. These people were all being held prisoner at Son Tay.

In the months of preparation, more photos were taken of the area. It looked like many of the prisoners had been moved

to another location. But Simons and his team continued with their operation.

Berets rushed into the camp. They killed or wounded many enemies. But the photos were true. The prisoners had been moved. No Americans were found at Son Tay. Simons called for the Berets to get out. As swiftly as they had arrived, the Berets left.

No prisoners were rescued that night. But that didn't mean the Berets' operation was not successful. No U.S. troops were lost in the 27-minute raid. It serves as a perfect example of the speed and strength of the Green Berets.

◄ **To prepare and help train for the operation, Green Berets studied a model of the Son Tay prison camp.**

CHAPTER 3

OPERATION JUST CAUSE

T hree U.S. Black Hawk helicopters roared into the skies of Panama. The year was 1989. A sudden blast of enemy gunfire flew past them. None of the helicopters were hit. The Green Berets had received information. It said that a **convoy** of Panama soldiers was headed for the Pacora River Bridge in Panama. Panama had declared war against the United States. The U.S. military decided to **invade** Panama. The Pacora River Bridge was one of the key targets. It was a great place to hide and initiate an attack.

The Berets needed to take the Pacora River Bridge. To do so, they had to get there before the convoy arrived. Bullets from the convoy whizzed past the Black Hawk helicopters. But the Berets did not change their mission. Within no time, the Black Hawks were at the bridge. As the helicopters soared overhead, soldiers spied the convoy. The first truck of the convoy was on the bridge. The Berets wasted no time.

BA-BOOM! The missile struck the truck. But the truck continued to move. The Berets called in a **gunship**. A glint of silver in the sky, the flying gunship fired its massive guns.

The convoy's lead vehicle was destroyed, and the convoy **retreated**. But then it made a second attack. The Green Berets fended it off again. They forced the enemy to retreat for good. U.S. forces had the Pacora River Bridge under control.

Panama surrendered to U.S. forces. Operation Just Cause was a success. It brought about a new style of military methods. These involved careful planning, focused training, and speedy execution.

CHAPTER 4

OPERATION VIKING HAMMER

Green eyes glowed in the night. Shadows of Green Beret soldiers moved as one along the jagged ridges of the mountains. Thin stones cracked beneath their feet and a freezing wind cut through their gear. It was a cold March night in Iraq in 2003.

Suddenly, from above, a missile streaked across the night sky. *KA-BOOM!*

The ground shook, and the flickering light of an explosion bathed their faces in a red and yellow glow. The ground beneath their feet trembled. Smoke rose from the destroyed buildings above.

The mountaintop region of northern Iraq—known as Iraq Kurdistan—was held by a **terrorist** group known as Ansar Al-Islam. This spot gave the terrorists a view of the whole area. It was up to Special Forces Green Berets to fight off Ansar Al-Islam. The Berets needed to open the border. Then soldiers from the area could join the battle against the terrorists.

Along the mountain ridge, more flashes of light lit up the night like fireworks. Operation Viking Hammer had begun. Small groups of soldiers were told to eliminate the enemies in the mountains. The Green Berets flew at dangerously low levels through the night. When they landed, they split into units. Kurdish rebels would be joining each unit in the fight.

Officials at the White House watched video of the invasion as the teams moved toward the mountains. As they got close, Al-Islam forces fired from their snowy peaks. The Berets were pinned down. They called for an **airstrike**. A pair of fighter planes roared overhead. They dropped bombs and rained bullets down on the enemy. The gunfire stopped, and the Americans moved forward.

The Berets destroyed enemy positions. They raided houses and collapsed caves. The skills they used in Operation Viking

▲ Ansar Al-Islam settled in the mountains, giving them a great view of oncoming forces.

▲ Two F-18 fighter planes flew in for an airstrike.

Hammer took the enemy by surprise. For two days, the units attacked Al-Islam. Finally the enemy retreated. The Green Berets had another victory.

CHAPTER 5

OPERATION ENDURING FREEDOM

t was 2011 in Afghanistan. Enemy fighters known as the Taliban had seized control of the Chamkani District Center building. They had set up position inside and had begun firing at a nearby U.S. post. Chamkani had been a place of great conflict. The small Special Forces base was located among rugged peaks.

The Taliban fighters fired. Their bullets rained down from the building onto the Special Forces. U.S. Chief Warrant Officer Jason Myers assembled a five-man team to stop the enemy. Two members of the team were Special Forces soldiers. The other three members were Afghan police officers. Green Berets had trained these officers to fight alongside them. The Green Berets secured the entrance to the building. The soldiers entered the building's lobby.

Rat-a-tat-a-tat!

The Taliban fired back. Green Beret Sergeant First Class Matthew Brown lobbed a grenade. He hoped it would clear the room in the compound. But swirling dust from its explosion made it difficult to see.

Suddenly, coming at him through the dust was another grenade.

Brown caught the grenade. He threw it into the corner of the lobby. Then he dove at an Afghan officer to shield him as the grenade exploded.

BOOM!

Another grenade shook the doorway as an injured Myers took out the enemy. Then he ordered the team to get out.

Gunfire continued outside. Brown met with two other Afghan officers. They waited for help to come. The mountains and cliffs around Chamkani made it hard for helicopters to land or offer air support. The Special Forces stationed in the village had no transport, supplies, or help when the Taliban attacked.

Special Forces rescued nine hostages from the district center building. Five additional hostages were rescued from the second floor. Fifteen hours later, the hostages were safe. Myers led a team that made sure the building was clear.

◀ Special Forces are taught how to handle and throw grenades.

GLOSSARY

airstrike (AIR-strike): An airstrike is an attack or bombing made from the air. The airstrike dropped a number of bombs on the enemy's hideout.

convoy (KAHN-voi): A convoy is a group of vehicles that travel together. The convoy traveled together for safety.

gunship (GUHN-ship): A gunship is an aircraft with guns or cannons. The gunship dropped bombs on the enemy.

hostage (HAH-stij): A hostage is someone who is kept prisoner until the captor gets what they demand. The Green Berets rescued each hostage.

invade (in-VADE): To invade is to enter a country in order to conquer it. Soldiers will invade the country.

recruit (ri-KROOT): A recruit is a person who has recently joined the armed forces. The recruit trained to become a Green Beret.

retreated (ri-TREET-ud): Retreated means to have moved back or withdrawn from a difficult situation. The enemies retreated after the Green Berets fired.

terrorist (TER-ur-ist): A terrorist is a person who uses violence and threats to gain power or force a government to do something. A terrorist group attacked New York City on September 11, 2001.

TO LEARN MORE

Books

Bozzo, Linda. *Green Berets*. Mankato, MN: Amicus High
    Interest, 2015.

Rose, Simon. *Green Berets*. New York: AV2 by Weigl, 2014.

Whiting, Jim. *Green Berets*. Mankato, MN: Creative
    Education, 2015.

Web Sites

Visit our Web site for links about missions of the U.S. Green
Berets: childsworld.com/links

*Note to Parents, Teachers, and Librarians: We routinely verify our Web links to make sure
they are safe and active sites. So encourage your readers to check them out!*

SELECTED BIBLIOGRAPHY

Gargus, John. *The Son Tay Raid: American POWs in Vietnam
    Were Not Forgotten*. College Station: TX: Texas A&M
    University, 2007.

McKinney, Mike, and Mike Ryan. *Chariots of the Damned:
    Helicopter Special Operations from Vietnam to Kosovo*.
    New York: Thomas Dunne Books, 2002.

McManners, Hugh. *Ultimate Special Forces*. New York:
    Metro Books, 2011.

Robinson, Linda. *Masters of Chaos: The Secret History of the
    Special Forces*. New York: PublicAffairs, 2004.

Ryan, Mike. *Special Operations in Iraq*. Barnsley, South
    Yorkshire: Pen & Sword Military, 2004.

INDEX

ABOUT THE AUTHOR

Brandon Terrell is the author of numerous children's books, with topics ranging from sports to spooky stories to swashbuckling adventures. When not hunched over his laptop writing, Brandon enjoys watching movies, reading, and spending time with his wife and two children.